A MASKED
FAIRY TALE

GOLDILOCKS
AND THE THREE BEARS

Illustrated by Ellie Jenkins

Kane Miller
A DIVISION OF EDC PUBLISHING

ONCE
UPON A TIME,

there was a **delightful** young girl named Goldilocks.

Well, Goldilocks wasn't THAT delightful... she was actually very **naughty** and very, **VERY fussy.**

One morning, Goldilocks went for a walk in the forest. It didn't take long until she was BORED.

There were no toys,
no TV shows and
NO VIDEO GAMES
in the forest.

Goldilocks had no idea what to do, so she climbed a big tree.

Off in the distance was a fluffy plume of smoke.

Goldilocks sniffed and sniffed.

"OOooooooooooooh!"
she cooed, licking her lips greedily.

"WHO SMELLS PORRIDGE?"

Goldilocks **LOVED** warm delicious porridge!

Goldilocks shimmied down the big tree and followed her nose.

Soon, she reached a sweet little cottage that smelled like warm delicious porridge.

Goldilocks knocked on the door.

Knock!

Knock!

Knock! Knock!

Knockety-Knockety-KNOCKETY!

KNOCK-KNOCK!

KNOCK!

When nobody answered the door, Goldilocks **crept** inside.
(She was very naughty, remember?)

Three bowls of porridge sat on the kitchen table.

First, Goldilocks tasted the **BiG** bowl of porridge. It was too hot.

Then, Goldilocks tasted the **MiDDLE-SiZED** bowl of porridge.
It was too cold.

Finally, Goldilocks tasted the LITTLE bowl of porridge. It was **JUST RIGHT!**

SLURP!

Goldilocks gobbled the LITTLE bowl of porridge and licked the bowl clean.

Burp.

Remember how we said that Goldilocks was very naughty?
Well, she was also a terrible **SNOOP!**

"I wonder what's in the next room?" she said.
There, Goldilocks found three chairs and an

ENORMOUS TV.

First, Goldilocks sat in the **BiG** chair. It was too **HARD.**

Then, Goldilocks sat in the **MIDDLE-SIZED** chair. It was too soft.

Finally, Goldilocks sat in the LITTLE chair. It was **JUST RIGHT!**

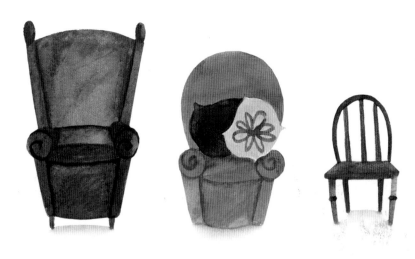

But wait!

The little chair **CREAKED** a little... **CROAKED** a little...

and, uh-oh...

CRACKED INTO PIECES!

"Oops!" said Goldilocks.

All this snooping was EXHAUSTING, so Goldilocks wandered upstairs, looking for somewhere to rest. There, she found a bedroom with three neat beds.

First, Goldilocks lay in the BIG bed. It was too **HARD.**

Then, Goldilocks lay in the **MIDDLE-SIZED** bed. It was too soft.

Finally, Goldilocks lay in the LITTLE bed. It was **JUST RIGHT!**

Goldilocks fell sound asleep.

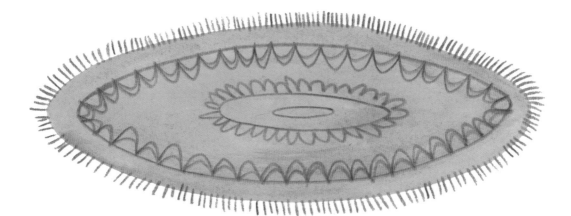

While Goldilocks slept, the three bears that lived in the cottage came home from their morning walk.

"Porridge! Porridge! Porridge! YUM! YUM! YUM!" they sang.

But something wasn't quite right...

"Who's been eating my **BIG** bowl of porridge?" thundered Papa Bear.

"Who's been eating my **MIDDLE-SIZED** bowl of porridge?" gasped Mama Bear.

"And who's been eating my LITTLE bowl of porridge... and gobbled it all up?" sighed Baby Bear.

Next, the three bears walked into the living room to watch their favorite TV show.

But something wasn't quite right...

"Who's been sitting in my BIG chair?" thundered Papa Bear.

"Who's been sitting in my MIDDLE-SIZED chair?" gasped Mama Bear.

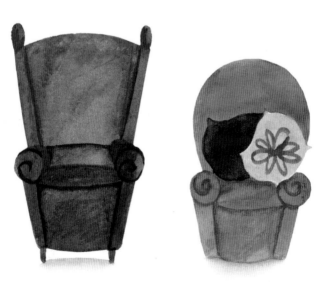

"And who's been sitting in my LITTLE chair... and

broken it to pieces?"

wailed Baby Bear.

ZZZZZZZZZZZZZZZZZZZ.

SHAKE.

Goldilocks's snores were so loud they made the cottage SHAKE.

The three bears raced upstairs. They were surprised
to find a little girl asleep in Baby Bear's bed!

Mama Bear gently patted Goldilocks's golden hair.

**"Do your mama and papa know
where you are?"** she asked kindly.

But Goldilocks didn't speak bear language.
All she heard when she woke up was,

"GRRRRRRRRRRRRRR!"

Without a word, Goldilocks LEAPT out of Baby Bear's bed,
Slid down the stairs and **skidded** out the door.

After that, Goldilocks NEVER
crept into empty cottages EVER AGAIN.

(And the three bears always ate porridge <u>before</u> their morning walk.)

First American Edition 2017
Kane Miller, A Division of EDC Publishing

Text, illustrations and design copyright © 2016 Hardie Grant Egmont
First published in Australia by Hardie Grant Egmont 2016

For information contact:
Kane Miller, A Division of EDC Publishing
PO Box 470663
Tulsa, OK 74147-0663
www.kanemiller.com
www.edcpub.com
www.usbornebooksandmore.com

Library of Congress Control Number: 2016943262

Printed in China
1 2 3 4 5 6 7 8 9 10

ISBN: 978-1-61067-609-0